Barney's Christmas Wishes

PUFFIN BOOKS

Dear Parents

Young children love the winter holiday season, especially the tradition of exchanging gifts. In this heartwarming story, BJ and Baby Bop experience the joy of giving and learn that it is as rewarding as receiving.

We consider books to be lifelong gifts that develop and encourage the love of reading. We hope you enjoy reading along with Barney, BJ and Baby Bop. Happy Christmas!

Mary Ann Dudko, Ph.D.
Margie Larsen, M.Ed.
Early Childhood Education Specialists

Art Director: Tricia Legault
Designer: Nelson Greenfield

PUFFIN BOOKS

Published by the Penguin Group under licence from Lyons Partnership, L.P.
Penguin Books Ltd, 27 Wrights Lane, London W8 5TZ, England
Penguin Putnam Inc., 375 Hudson Street, New York, New York 10014, USA
Penguin Books Australia Ltd, Ringwood, Victoria, Australia
Penguin Books Canada Ltd, 10 Alcorn Avenue, Toronto, Ontario, Canada M4V 3B2
Penguin Books (NZ) Ltd, 182–190 Wairau Road, Auckland 10, New Zealand

Penguin Books Ltd, Registered Offices: Harmondsworth, Middlesex, England

First published in the USA by Barney™ Publishing, a division of Lyons Partnership, L.P. 1997
Published in Great Britain in Puffin Books 1998
10 9 8 7 6 5 4 3 2 1

Barney's™ Christmas Wishes

Written by Stephen White
Illustrated by Darren McKee

Once upon a fun, frosty December day, Barney hung a beautiful new Christmas wreath on the front door. "There!" he said happily. "Now I'm all ready for Christmas!"

"I'm not ready yet," said BJ. "I still have something important to do!"
"So do I!" laughed Baby Bop.

Back inside the house, BJ hung colourful pictures of stars and planets around his room. "Great!" said BJ. "If I get a toy robot for Christmas, my room will be all ready!"

In her room, Baby Bop made a doll's house out of a cardboard box. She even put her blankey inside to make it warm and cosy.

"Look what I've done!" said Baby Bop. "If I get a doll for Christmas, my room will be all ready!"

"Getting presents is a lot of fun," said Barney, "but it's also very nice to give." Then he smiled and said, "And I've got a surprise to give you right now! We're all going to visit Father Christmas!"

"How will we get there?" asked BJ.
Barney replied, "Just look outside!"
"It's Father Christmas's sleigh!" Baby Bop
shouted happily. "And there are real reindeer!"

The sleigh flew through the night sky, soaring high over houses, trees and even mountains!

"Whee!" laughed Baby Bop as she jingled the sleigh bells. "This is fun!"

"Hey, look!" said BJ. "I can see the North Pole!"

"And I can see my very good friend, Father Christmas!" Barney said happily.

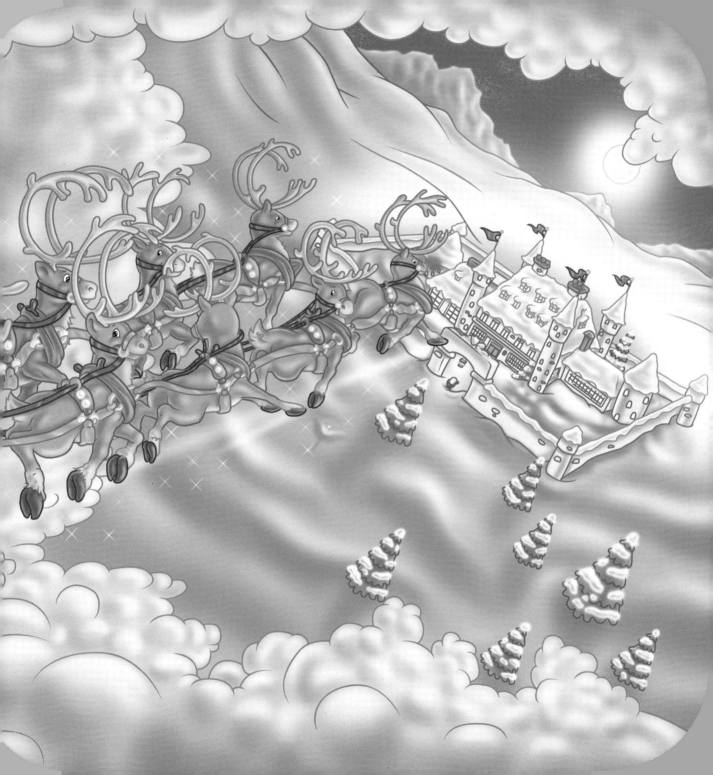

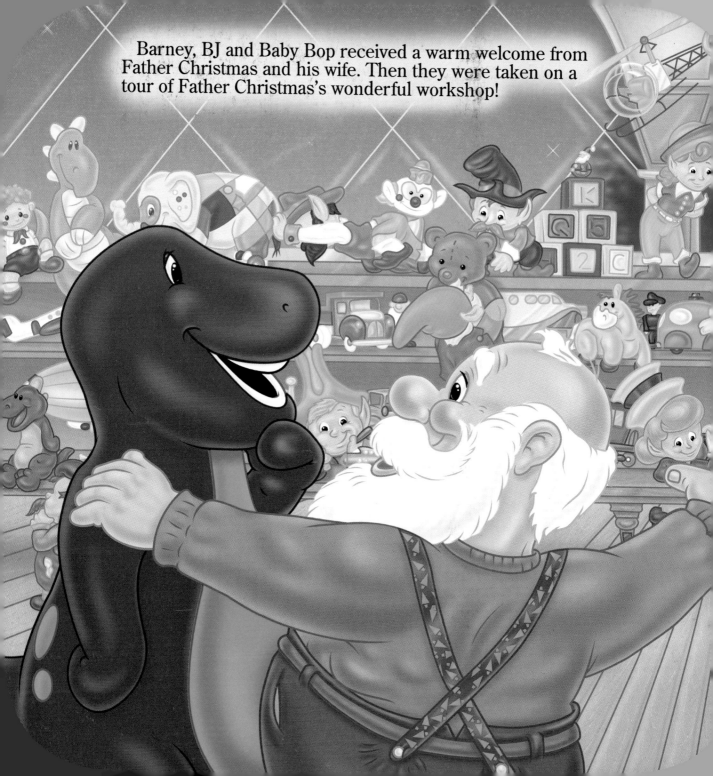

Barney, BJ and Baby Bop received a warm welcome from Father Christmas and his wife. Then they were taken on a tour of Father Christmas's wonderful workshop!

"It's stuuuu-pendous!" laughed Barney. Everywhere they looked, BJ and Baby Bop saw happy elves working on toys.

"We're making more toys than usual this year," Father Christmas said with a smile, "because so many boys and girls have been good!"

In another part of Father Christmas's workshop, elves wrapped toys in Christmas paper and tied them with a rainbow of ribbons!

At the end of the tour, Father Christmas settled into his favourite chair. "Baby Bop," he asked, "what is the one present you'd like most for Christmas?"

Baby Bop thought and thought.
"I know!" she giggled. Then she
whispered in Father Christmas's ear.

Next, Father Christmas asked what present BJ wanted most for Christmas. BJ thought about it and then whispered in Father Christmas's other ear.

"Ho-ho-ho!" Father Christmas laughed. "You've both made very good choices!"

When their visit with Father Christmas was over, Barney, BJ and Baby Bop returned home. And just a few days later … it was Christmas morning!

"Look!" said Baby Bop. "We have presents from Father Christmas!"

"I'm sure they'll be very special!" said Barney. "Why don't you open yours first, Baby Bop?"

Baby Bop opened her present and held it up for everyone to see.
"Wow!" said BJ. "It's a toy robot – just what *I* wanted!"
"That's what I asked Father Christmas for!" Baby Bop giggled.

"Why did you ask for a toy robot?" said Barney.
Baby Bop smiled as she gave the toy robot to BJ. "So I
could give it to my favourite brother!" she said happily.

Next, BJ opened his present and held it up for
everyone to see.

"Oh, look!" said Baby Bop. "It's a doll – just
what *I* wanted!"

"That's what I asked Father Christmas for!" laughed BJ.

"And why did you ask for a doll?" Barney asked
BJ with a smile.

BJ put the cuddly doll into Baby Bop's arms. "So I
could give it to my favourite sister!" he said.

"You see?" said Barney. "It really is nice to give things to others!"

And to prove it, Barney gave something very special to BJ and Baby Bop – a great big Christmas hug!